for Cuffy and Trev and Emily and
Rachel and Gretchen and Alex and J·L
and Stone and Hamish and Bones
and Cooper and Reevsey

First published in Great Britain in 1995
by Orion Children's Books
a division of the Orion Publishing Group Ltd
Orion House
5 Upper St Martin's Lane
London WC2H 9EA

Copyright © Selina Young 1995

The right of Selina Young to be identified as
the author of this work has been asserted.

A catalogue record for this book
is available from the British Library
Printed in Italy
ISBN 1 85881 107 4

Tiger the cat   Adam's Grandpa   Adam's Grandma   Kevin   Julie Adam's babysitter   Adam Pig's Dad   Tom   Angela

Adam Pig's BIG book

SELINA YOUNG

Orion
Children's Books

the playgroup leader Mrs Nib   Robert   Adam's baby sister Lisa   Adam Pig's Mum   Winnie   Adam Pig   These are my family and friends!   Fred the dog

Hi! I'm Adam Pig and this is what is in my Big Book!

Look what Adam Pig can do

he can pat the dog

he can ride his trike very fast!

he can paint a picture

Whoops! look at all the mess Adam's made!

he can do a puzzle

he can jump up and down

he can kick a ball

10

he can
look at a book

he can
touch his toes

he can
hop on one foot

he can play in his
paddling pool

he can make a fort
out of bricks

he can push his wheelbarrow

I can
do all this.
What
can you do?

Adam Pig goes shopping

Mum was writing a shopping list. She needed apples, bread, baked beans, washing powder, milk, yoghurt and toilet paper. Adam Pig looked in the cupboard. He thought Mum needed biscuits, crisps and fizzy drinks. Mum put the list in her bag. Then she and Adam went to the supermarket.

At the supermarket Mum got a big trolley.

Adam Pig sat in the front. He held the shopping list
and Mum pushed the trolley.

Mum put the things they
needed in the trolley.

Adam Pig put his things
in the trolley too!

When Mum had got all the things on the list she pushed the trolley with all the shopping and Adam to the checkout.

"I wonder who put these things in?" said Mum, picking up the biscuits, crisps and fizzy drinks. Mum said Adam could choose one thing, but the rest must go back. Adam Pig chose a fizzy drink.

She got out her purse and paid the lady. The lady gave Adam Pig the bill.

At home Adam helped Mum unpack the shopping. He took out a loaf of bread, a pint of milk, one box of washing powder, two tins of baked beans, three red apples, four rolls of toilet paper and five pots of yoghurt. Adam Pig had been so helpful shopping that Mum gave him one of the red apples to have with his fizzy drink.

"I like shopping," said Adam.

15

Build a car
with Adam Pig

a cardboard box big enough to sit in

five paper plates

scissors

paint and brushes

glue

Get a grown-up to help you cut out two door shapes in the sides of the box.

Stick on four of the paper plates to make the wheels.

Then paint the car in bright colours. Mix the paint with some glue to make it stick. Cover up any writing on the box.

Vroom vroom!

Adam Pig uses the last paper plate as a steering wheel. Now he can race off in his new car.

Adam Pig's baby sister

Adam Pig has a baby sister called Lisa. He helps Mum push Lisa in her buggy. He likes watching Lisa have her bath.

He fetches the nappies and talcum powder so Mum can change the baby.

He gives Lisa
some of his toys
to play with.
Then he
brings her
her bottle.

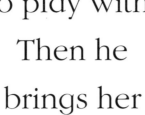

"What a help you are, Adam!" says Mum, and
she gives Adam Pig and Lisa a big hug.

Adam Pig goes to playgroup

Adam Pig was very excited.
It was his first day at playgroup.
Dad made him toast and jam
for breakfast. Mum helped Adam

button up his coat. Then

she took him to playgroup. She
gave him a big kiss goodbye.
Adam Pig waved to Mum
and went off with Mrs Nib.

"This is where we hang our coats," said Mrs Nib.
Another piglet held Adam's plane while he hung

his coat up.

There were lots of piglets at the playgroup. They were all busy having fun. Adam soon forgot to miss his Mum. Mrs Nib showed Adam all sorts of things to do.

He painted a picture with Kevin, played dressing up with Winnie,

made a dinosaur out of blocks with Angela, and helped Robert and Tom tidy up ready for the story.

All the piglets sat down to hear Mrs Nib read the story.

Afterwards, Winnie and Kevin helped Mrs Nib hand out biscuits and milk.

Soon all the mums and dads started arriving to pick up their piglets. Mum came to pick Adam Pig up.

"Bye," called Adam to his new friends.

"Don't forget your painting, Adam," said Mrs Nib. Adam gave his painting to Mum.

"Thank you, Adam. Aren't you clever!" said Mum. When they got home Adam helped Mum stick his painting on the fridge with four shiny magnets.

leaf prints

Paint your leaves in bright colours. Then press the painted leaves on the paper to get your leaf print.

potato prints

Get Mum to halve a potato and cut out a raised shape. Paint the raised shape and print it on the paper.

sponge prints

Get help cutting up an old sponge. Dip the sponge pieces in different colours. You can make lots of patterns on the paper.

Adam.P.

Adam has used leaves, potatoes and bits of sponge to make a big picture.

Adam Pig's favourite toys

building blocks

colouring book and crayons

jack in the box

boat

jigsaw

aeroplane

tipper truck

teddy

What are your favourite toys?

train set

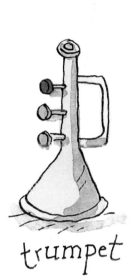

trumpet

bucket, spade and rake

robot

tool set

Adam Pig's friend

Adam Pig's
friend Kevin
had come to tea.
They were playing
with Adam Pig's
trainset.

"I want to
play with the
engine," said
Kevin.

"You can't!"
said Adam.
"It's mine, I
want it!"

28

"Shhh! What's all this noise?" said Mum. "Why don't you build a big train with lots of carriages and take turns pushing it?"

Adam Pig and Kevin made a track for their big train to go on. It was much more fun than fighting.

Adam Pig helps in the garden

Adam Pig likes visiting his Grandpa. Grandpa has a big garden and there is always lots to do. Today Adam was helping Grandpa plant his vegetables.

"Spring is the best time for planting seeds," said Grandpa.

First Adam Pig helped Grandpa with the digging. When the vegetable patch was ready, Grandpa made little holes for Adam Pig to put the seeds in.

They planted lettuces,
carrots, tomatoes
and beans.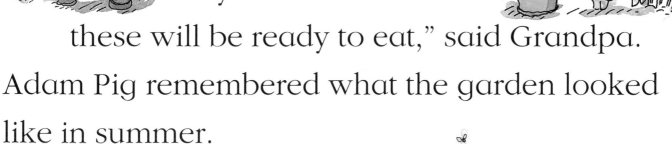

"By summer time all
these will be ready to eat," said Grandpa.

Adam Pig remembered what the garden looked
like in summer.

All the flowers were out and the sun was hot.
He would hunt for caterpillars and butterflies
and play under the sprinkler.

In autumn all the leaves
turned yellow and orange and fell
off the trees. Adam would help Grandpa to rake
them up into big piles. They were fun to play in.
In winter the snow would come and Adam and
Grandpa would wrap up warm
and build snow pigs and
throw snowballs.

Grandma gave Adam breadcrumbs to put on the bird table.

When Grandpa and Adam had planted all the seeds, they went inside for lunch.

"It won't be long before we'll be eating the vegetables you helped plant," said Grandpa. Adam Pig could hardly wait for summer!

This is what you need

Grow a bean with Adam Pig

runner bean seeds

SEEDS RUNNER BEANS

an empty jam jar

blotting paper

watering can

First soak the blotting paper in water. Then put it in the jam jar.

Put one runner bean seed in the jam jar on the wet blotting paper.

Make sure the blotting paper stays wet. Give your bean seed a little water each day. Soon the seed will start to grow.

Look how much Adam Pig's runner bean has grown!

Adam Pig's babysitter

"This is Julie. She's going to babysit for you and Lisa while Mum and I go out," Dad told Adam Pig.

"Would you like to play a game?" asked Julie.

Adam didn't want to play any games. He wanted his Mum and Dad back.

"Mum said you planted a seed in a jar," said Julie. "May I see it?"

Adam showed Julie the little shoot that had sprouted from his bean seed.

Then Julie read Adam and Lisa their favourite story. Adam didn't mind having a babysitter at all.

37

Help Adam Pig get dressed

woolly hat

stripy top

swimming trunks

T-shirt

vest

Y-fronts

Shorts

bow tie

mittens

knitted top

socks

CHEST of DRAWERS

spotty trousers

pyjamas

Adam Pig goes to the park

Mum helped Adam Pig put on his coat and scarf. He was going to the park.

Mum and Adam waited at the bus stop for the bus.

"Here it comes!" shouted Adam, jumping up and down. Mum bought a bus ticket. Adam Pig sat by the window. As the bus drove along he saw a spotty dog, a piglet on a bike, and a lady with lots of shopping.

Adam Pig's friends were in the park too.

"Hello, Adam," they said.

"Hello," said Adam.

Adam Pig queued
with them to go
on the slide.

One, two, three,
whooosh!

They swung on the swings, and whizzed round
and round on the roundabout.

Adam Pig was hot after all that whizzing!

Afterwards they played hide-and-seek and chase.

"Adam," called Mum.

"It's time to
go home."

"I don't want to!"
said Adam.

But Mum said they
had to go, or they
would miss the bus.

"Where's your scarf, Adam?" asked Mum. Oh dear! Where had Adam left it?

Adam's friends helped him look for the scarf.

Then Adam remembered he had left it on the roundabout. He ran over.

"Hurry!" said Mum. "Or we'll miss the bus."

Mum and Adam ran as fast as they could to the bus stop. They were just in time to catch the bus home.

Make a sock puppet with Adam Pig

First get a grown-up to help you cut out two eye shapes and a tongue from the coloured felt.

Glue the eyes near the toe of the sock.

Sssssss!

Then turn the sock over and glue on the tongue. When the glue is dry, your puppet is ready to use.

Adam Pig calls his sock puppet Sid.

Adam Pig's favourite food

ice lolly

cornflakes and milk

bananas

milkshake

cheese

crisps

water-melon

carrots

chocolate

milk

biscuits

jelly

vegetable soup

spaghetti

orange juice

oranges

yoghurt

pasta shapes

boiled eggs

french fries

porridge

fizzy drinks

raisins

crunchy apples

cheese and tomato
sandwiches

popcorn

toast and jam

baked beans
on toast

strawberries
and cream

jacket potato
with cheese

what
do you
like to eat?

47

Adam Pig's birthday Party

Today was Adam Pig's birthday. He was having a party. All his friends had been sent invitations.

Adam helped Mum set the table for his birthday tea. He helped Dad blow up the balloons. When everything was ready, Mum helped Adam into his party clothes.

Soon his friends arrived. They all had birthday
presents for Adam!
Grandpa and Grandma
arrived with an extra
big present.

Adam sat down with all his parcels.

"Thank you, everyone!"
he said when he had
opened everything.
"Let's have tea." said Mum.
All the piglets sat up at the table.
There was lots to eat: cheese rolls, carrot sticks,
flapjacks, crisps, apple tarts
and heaps more.

When everyone had finished Mum brought in the
cake. Dad lit the candles.

"Happy birthday to you," sang everyone to Adam
Pig. Adam blew out the four
candles with a big puff.

After tea there were party
games. Adam and his friends
played musical chairs, pass the parcel,
and pin the tail on the donkey.
Poor Kevin hadn't won a
prize in any of the games.
"Let's have another
round of pass the
parcel." said Dad.

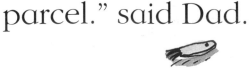

This time Kevin won a pack of coloured pencils.

When it was time to go, Adam's Mum gave

everyone a slice of birthday cake to take home.

Adam's Dad gave each piglet a balloon.

"Bye!" said Adam Pig.

"Thanks for having us,"

said Adam's friends as

they waved goodbye.

Adam Pig likes helping

He helps do the vacuuming

He brings the post in

He helps brush the dog

He helps Mum to bake a cake

He helps Grandpa find his glasses

He helps feed the cat

He helps Dad wash the car

What do you do to help?

One morning when Adam Pig woke up, he didn't feel very well. He was covered in spots!

Mum took him straight to the doctor's. The doctor looked at Adam's spots.

He listened to Adam's heart with his stethoscope. "Thump, thump," it went.

Then he took Adam's temperature. "You've got chickenpox," said the doctor. He gave Adam some cream to put on the spots.

Mum tucked Adam up in bed. "You'll soon feel better," said Mum. And he did!

Adam Pig's bedtime

Adam Pig had had tea and was watching cartoons. "After this one it's bathtime," said Mum.

Adam Pig liked baths, especially bubble baths. While Mum turned on the taps Adam Pig poured in lots of bubble bath. "Not too much, Adam!" said Mum.

Mum scrubbed Adam all over with a big yellow sponge. He shut his eyes tight so as not to get soap in them.

Adam played with his boats while Mum went and fetched his pyjamas. She wrapped Adam up in a big fluffy towel. When he was quite dry she puffed on some talcum powder. Adam hopped into his pyjamas. "Don't forget to clean your teeth," said Mum. Adam squeezed out lots of stripy toothpaste on to his toothbrush to make sure his teeth got extra clean.

Adam Pig was all ready for bed.
He went downstairs to say
goodnight to everyone.
"Night Grandma,
night Grandpa,
night Lisa,
night Dad,
night Mum,
night Tiger,
night Fred."

Adam Pig wasn't tired.
"I might get sleepy if
Dad read me a story,"
said Adam.
"Just one,"
said Dad.

Adam Pig thought
that one story
would be fine if
Mum could come up
and tuck him in.

Adam picked a book for Dad to read.

Mum snuggled him into bed, while Dad began the story. Adam Pig was so warm and cosy that he didn't hear Dad read the last few pages. He was fast asleep.